Make a Steampunk Crab!

John Burdess and Jonathon Phillips

Photographs by Lindsay Edwards

Contents

What Is Steampunk?

"Steampunk" is a **concept**, or idea, that first appeared in the novels of nineteenth-century writers such as Jules Verne. The introduction of machines powered by steam during the nineteenth century caused major changes in people's lives. Jules Verne was inspired by these changes and imagined a world that was completely steam powered – including cars, airships, and even computers!

French writer Jules Verne, one of the creators of steampunk, around 1892

Jules Verne imagined what airships would look like if they were powered by steam.

Since then, there have been many novels, TV shows, comics, movies and video games that use steampunk as their "look". To make the steampunk style come alive, things are made to look like parts from steam-powered machines, and everyone wears a clothing style from over a hundred years ago.

a steam engine train in 1910

People dress up in steampunk fashion for festivals around the world, such as this music festival in England.

Steampunk can also be inspiration for making artworks and sculptures of the natural world. For example, an insect artwork could be made with springs and clockwork gears held together by bolts, or a turtle sculpture could be built as a steam-powered, **armoured** machine.

This sculpture in Russia was made in the steampunk style, using objects found on the street.

This fish is drawn in the steampunk style, with the gears of a machine shown inside.

Find out how to draw a **fictitious**, or make-believe, four-legged steampunk crab that has a steam engine chimney, a ship's portholes for eyes and giant, machine-like claws to pick objects up from the ocean floor.

Then, make a sculpture of a **metallic** steampunk crab that moves using magnets!

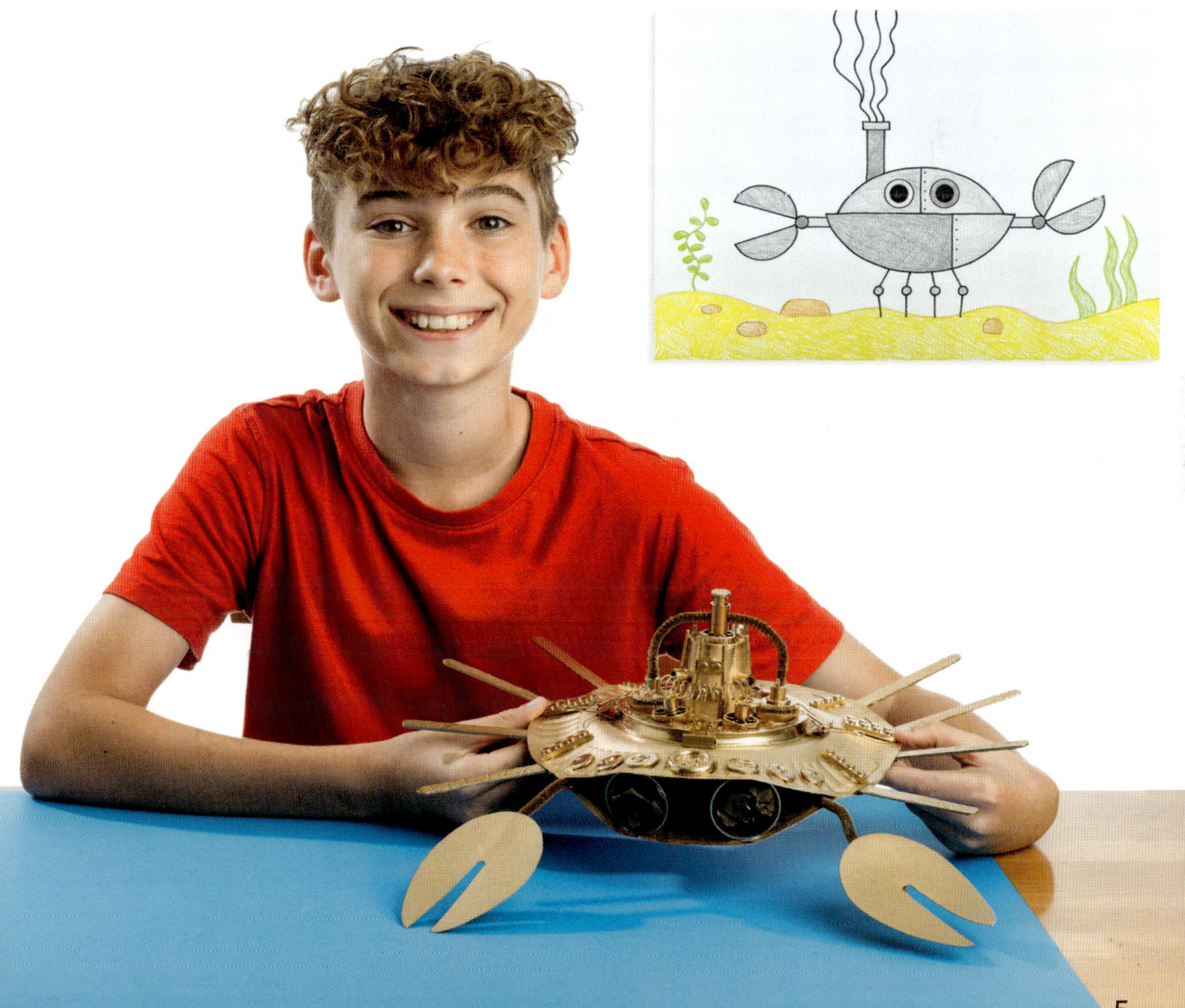

Draw a Steampunk Crab

Goal

To draw a crab in the steampunk style

Materials

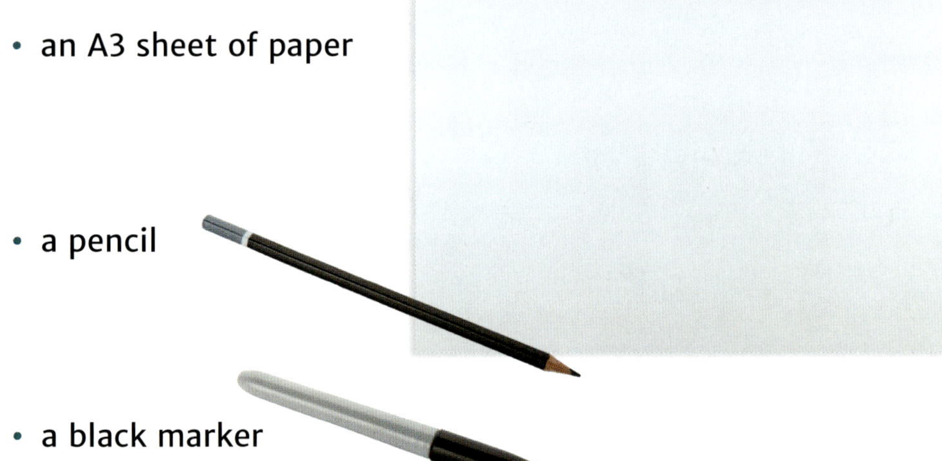

- an A3 sheet of paper
- a pencil
- a black marker
- an eraser
- coloured pencils or markers, including a silver or grey colour

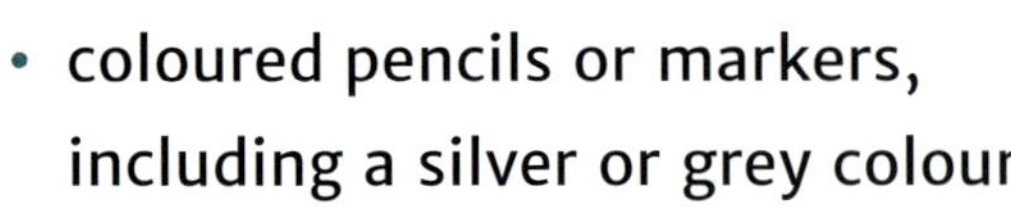

Steps

1. On the sheet of paper, use the pencil to draw half of a wide oval, with the flat, horizontal side at the bottom. This will be the crab's head.

2. Draw another half of an oval directly underneath the first one. Make the second one a little wider, with its flat side at the top, so that it shares the first oval's straight edge. This will be the crab's body.

3. Next, give the crab some eyes. In the top half-oval, draw two large circles. Then, draw a smaller circle inside each large one. To make the eyes look like a ship's portholes, colour in the smaller circles with the pencil.

a ship's porthole

4. To make your crab look like it is made of metal, draw two vertical lines to attach some "bolts" to. Draw one vertical line between the crab's eyes, from the top to the bottom of the crab's head. Then, draw another line anywhere from the middle of the crab down to the bottom of its body. Beside each vertical line, add a row of small dots to represent bolts.

5. Next, give your crab a steam engine chimney. Draw a narrow vertical rectangle coming out of the top of the crab, to the left of its eyes. To complete the chimney, add a smaller, horizontal rectangle on top of the vertical one. You may like to add some curly or wavy lines coming out of the top of the chimney to represent steam.

steam coming out of a train's chimney

6. Next, give your crab some mechanical legs. Draw a row of four small circles beneath the crab's body. Then, join those circles to the crab with four straight lines.

7. For the lower part of the crab's legs, draw four more short lines coming out from the bottom of the circles.

8. Finally, give your crab some mechanical claws. Draw two small horizontal rectangles touching the crab's body, one on each side. Add a small circle on the ends of those rectangles. Then, draw two half-ovals attached to each circle. Make the half-ovals look like claws by drawing them open wide at the end, with the flat edges facing inwards. *Snap! Snap!*

9. When you are happy with your design, trace over your pencil lines with the black marker. Then, erase any visible pencil marks.

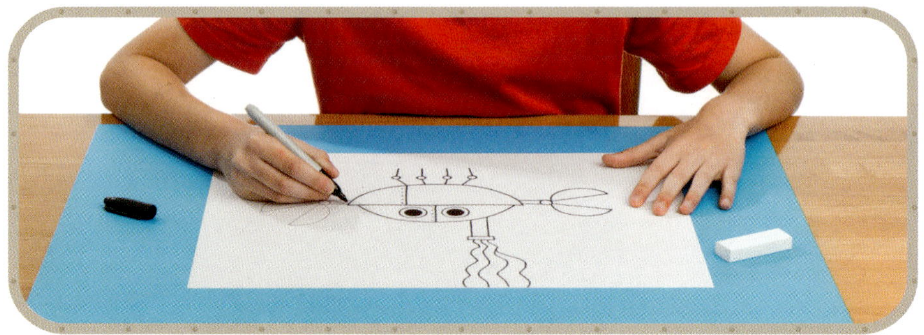

10. Last, use a silver or grey coloured pencil to colour in your crab. You may like to draw and colour in a sandy ocean floor and some seaweed using other coloured pencils.

There you have it – a steampunk crab!

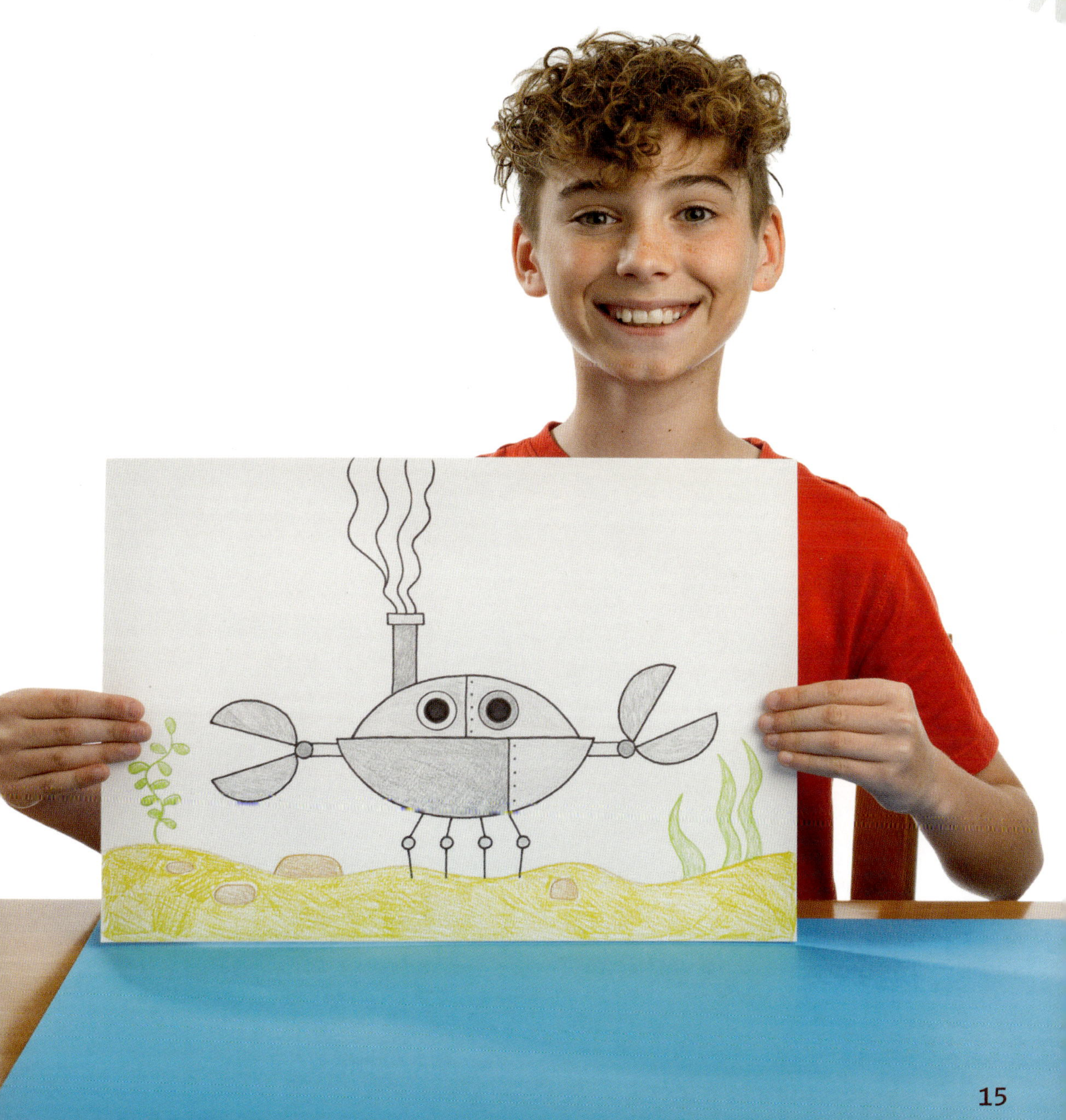

Build a Steampunk Crab

Goal

To build a sculpture of a crab in the steampunk style

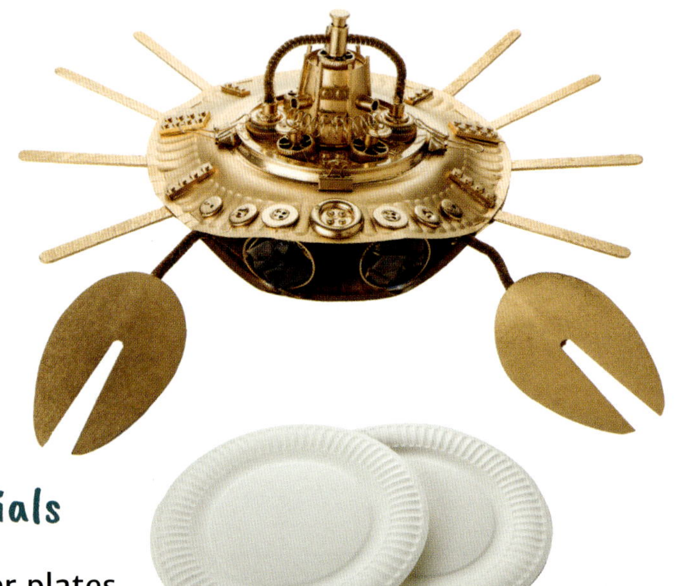

Materials

- 2 paper plates
- 8 craft sticks (paper straws, pencils or pipe cleaners could also be used)
- tape
- 2 pipe cleaners (craft sticks could also be used)
- an A5 piece of stiff white card

- a pencil

- scissors

- an A4 piece of black paper

- 2 bottle tops
- white glue
- a selection of **found objects** you can use to decorate your crab in a steampunk style, for example, buttons, wire or marker lids

- a stapler

- gold, silver or bronze metallic paint
- a paintbrush

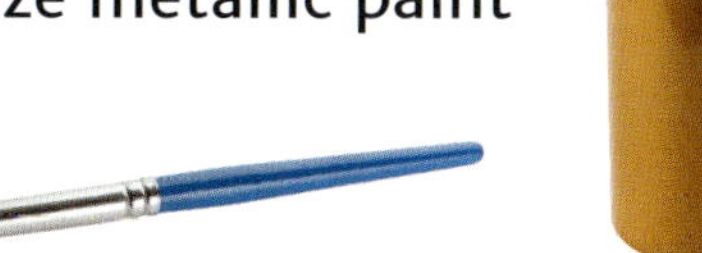

- a plastic container

Steps

1. First, make the crab's body and legs. Tape one end of the eight craft sticks to the top of one paper plate, four on each side.

2. On the white card, draw two oval-shaped crab claws with the pencil and cut them out. Tape the crab's claws onto two pipe cleaners. Then, tape the two pipe cleaners to the front of the crab's body.

3. Next, make the crab's eyes. Tear off a piece of the black paper, scrunch it up and glue it to the inside of one of the bottle tops. Repeat for the second eye.

4. Glue the bottle tops next to each other on the top of the paper plate, standing up on their sides at the front of the crab's body, and leave them to dry.

5. Next, make the crab's shell. Glue a selection of found objects to the bottom of the second paper plate. Leave it to dry.

When choosing your found objects, think about the steampunk style and what sorts of things are usually found in machines, for example, antennas, gears, **cogs**, **gauges**, chimneys, exhaust pipes, **hatches** and so on.

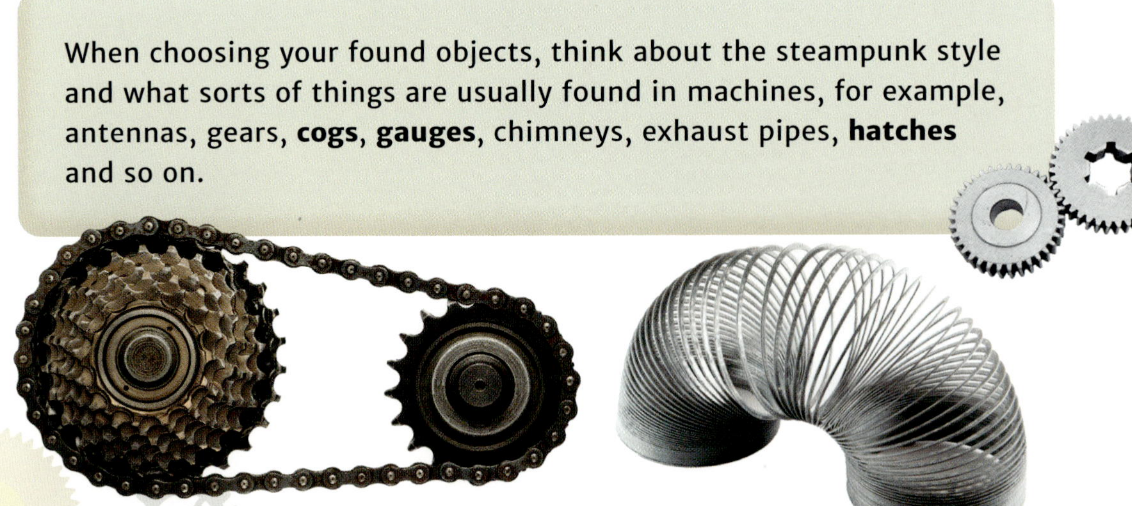

6. Once the glue on the crab's shell is dry, position the shell directly on top of the other paper plate, the crab's body. Staple the two plates together around the edge, including on either side of the eyes.

7. Use the paintbrush and the metallic paint to paint the crab, including the claws. Leave it to dry.

Your steampunk crab sculpture is complete!

Make Your Steampunk Crab Move!

Magnetism

This procedure uses **magnetism** to make the crab move. Magnetism is an invisible **force**. The area around a magnet is called a **magnetic field**. If you hold a material such as iron or steel close to a magnet, within its magnetic field, you will begin to feel the material and the magnet pull towards each other. Earth has its own magnetic field.

All magnets have a north-seeking **pole** and a south-seeking pole. If you place the north pole of one magnet against the south pole of another magnet, they will attract each other. If you try to put two poles of the same kind together, they will **repel** each other. This is how the steampunk crab sculpture will move.

Magnets normally have an "N" and an "S" on them, as well as different colours, to show which are the north and south poles.

Goal

To move your steampunk crab sculpture using magnetism

Materials

- a toy car

- 2 strong bar magnets with north and south poles of different colours (the magnets can be different sizes, but one should be small enough to fit on top of the toy car)

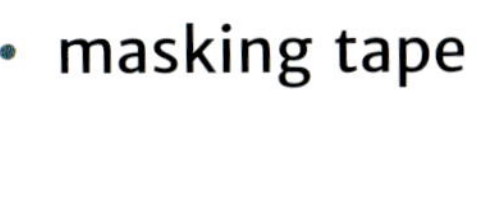

- masking tape
- a ruler
- scissors

Steps

1. Place the small magnet lengthwise on top of the toy car.
2. Use masking tape to attach the magnet to the top of the car. Make sure the tape is not covering the car's wheels.

3. Next, hide the car and the magnet underneath the crab's body. Use the ruler to measure a 15-centimetre length of tape. Loop it under the car and attach the ends to the underside of the crab.

4. Finally, make your steampunk crab move! Place your crab on the floor or another hard surface. Then, hold the second magnet about 5 centimetres away from your crab. Make sure you have the same poles matched together so the two magnets repel each other.

Watch as your steampunk crab moves away from the magnet!

Glossary

armoured (*adjective*)	covered or protected
cogs (*noun*)	parts of a machine that can move other parts to make the machine work
concept (*noun*)	an idea or a way of thinking
fictitious (*adjective*)	fake or invented
force (*noun*)	a power that can make things move
found objects (*noun*)	everyday things that normally would not be used in art
gauges (*noun*)	small tools, often a circle with a moving needle, that measure something
hatches (*noun*)	doors cut into floors or ceilings
magnetic field (*noun*)	the space around a magnet that is affected by it
magnetism (*noun*)	energy from a magnet that pushes and pulls
metallic (*adjective*)	like metal
pole (*noun*)	one of the two ends of a magnet that either pushes or pulls
repel (*verb*)	push away